A Red Fox Book

Published by Random House Children's Books
20 Vauxhall Bridge Road, London SW1V 2SA

A division of The Random House Group Ltd
London Melbourne Sydney Auckland
Johannesburg and agencies throughout the world

1 3 5 7 9 10 8 6 4 2

First published in Great Britain by Red Fox 2000

Printed in Singapore by Tien Wah Press (PTE) Ltd

THE RANDOM HOUSE GROUP Ltd Reg. No. 954009
www.randomhouse.co.uk

Into the
Woods

Nick Ward

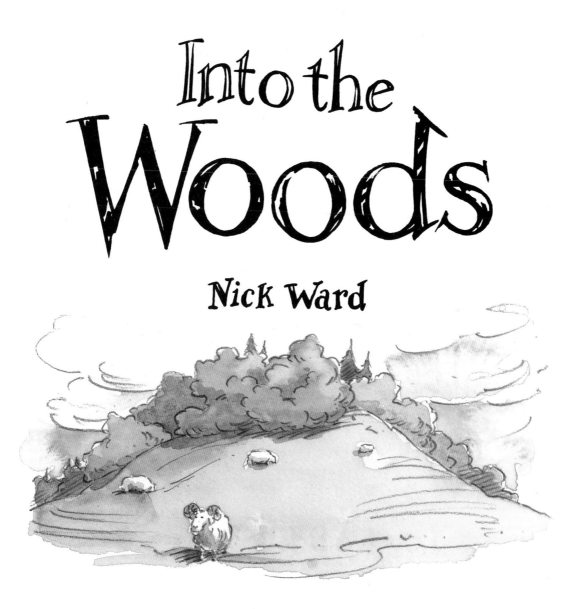

RED FOX

'Come on, you two,' said Grandpa, one morning. 'Let's go for a walk.'

'A walk?' yawned Emmy.

'Where to?' Charlie mumbled sleepily.

'Not far,' smiled Grandpa. 'Over the field and into the wood.'

'What's so special about a boring old wood?' grumbled Charlie, as they climbed the rickety stile into the meadow.

Grandpa chuckled. 'Why, the wood is a wonderful place.'

'It's a bit scary,' shivered Emmy, as they stepped into the shade of the trees. 'It feels old, Grandpa.'

'It's *very* old,' said Grandpa. 'Once upon a time, this wood covered almost the whole land.'

'Gosh!' gasped Charlie. 'It must have been enormous.'

'Huge!' laughed Grandpa. 'And not so very long ago, you might have seen a knight in armour ride his heavy horse over the field and into the wood.'

*T*hrough the morning mist he rides, tired from his long journey. Twigs crack beneath the huge feet of his horse.

'Look!' whispered Emmy, pointing to
where the mud was churned and pitted.
'Here are his hoof marks.'

'Maybe,' smiled Grandpa. 'Let's follow
them.'

Further into the musty wood they walked.

'Where would the knight be going, Grandpa?'
asked Charlie.

Mmm, Grandpa thought. 'Oh, but of course.
He would be searching for . . . a dragon. A fierce
and fiery dragon!' he said.

*C*amped by a pond, the knight chanced upon an old woodcutter. The woodcutter invited him to stop and share a meal.

As they ate, the knight talked of his difficult quest. The Queen had ordered him to capture a fierce and fiery dragon, but the knight had searched and searched without success.

'Over here, Grandpa,' called Charlie,
kicking over the ashes of a long-dead fire.
'This is where the knight stopped for his
breakfast!'

'Maybe,' smiled Grandpa. 'Let's go on.'

Further and further they walked, deep
into the heart of the wood. All was quiet
and mysterious.

*T*he woodcutter had not seen a dragon
for many years, so the knight
continued on his way. Watching and
listening, he urged his horse deep into the
heart of the wood.

A sudden noise made him turn . . . A
startled deer raced across his path, and
disappeared into the undergrowth. The
knight relaxed once more.

'Gosh, look out, Grandpa!' cried Emmy,
as a deer, nervous and quick, crashed
through the bracken ahead of them.

'Something's frightened her,' Grandpa
said.

'The knight,' murmured Charlie.

'Maybe,' said Grandpa.

They came to the edge of a large clearing. Trees had been broken and flattened. Some were charred. 'Where are we?' asked Charlie. It felt strange. Sort of secret.

'Well, well, well,' smiled Grandpa. 'I thought so!'

'What! What is it?'

'These are the remains of an old dragon's nest!'

*T*he knight rode to the edge of the clearing. A beautiful green dragon lay sleeping in the sun. At last! The knight's hand moved to the hilt of his sword. And then he stopped.

Three young dragons played close to their mother. They rolled and tumbled, chased and jumped. The knight's hand dropped from his sword, and he smiled. This time his Queen must go without.

'Fantastic,' said Charlie, as they started for home. 'A real dragon's nest.'

'Maybe,' Grandpa said.

But something was bothering Charlie. 'Do you think the knight caught the dragon?' he asked.

'No,' whispered Emmy. 'Look, Grandpa. Look!'

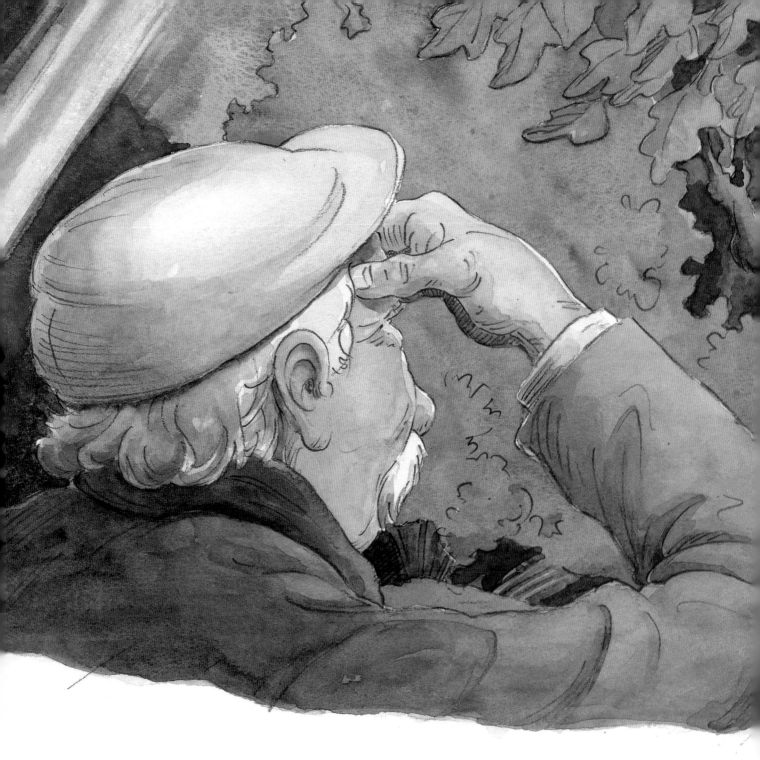

'Where, Emmy?' asked Grandpa, peering
into the gloom with his old eyes.

*T*he knight picked his lonely path back
through the trees.

'Didn't you see it?' asked the children.

'Maybe,' chuckled Grandpa. Out of the wood they walked, back into the early spring sunshine.

'I'm famished,' said Grandpa. 'Let's hurry home.'

*T*he knight gazed across the open fields.
Ahead lay the long journey home.
He would tell his queen the truth . . . that
there were no fierce or fiery dragons to be
found.

Some bestselling Red Fox picture books

THE BIG ALFIE AND ANNIE ROSE STORYBOOK
by Shirley Hughes
OLD BEAR
by Jane Hissey
JOHN PATRICK NORMAN McHENNESSY –
THE BOY WHO WAS ALWAYS LATE
by John Burningham
I WANT A CAT
by Tony Ross
NOT NOW, BERNARD
by David McKee
THE STORY OF HORRIBLE HILDA AND HENRY
by Emma Chichester Clark
THE SAND HORSE
by Michael Foreman and Ann Turnbull
BAD BORIS GOES TO SCHOOL
by Susie Jenkin-Pearce
MRS PEPPERPOT AND THE BILBERRIES
by Alf Prøysen
BAD MOOD BEAR
by John Richardson
WHEN SHEEP CANNOT SLEEP
by Satoshi Kitamura
THE LAST DODO
by Ann and Reg Cartwright
IF AT FIRST YOU DO NOT SEE
by Ruth Brown
THE MONSTER BED
by Jeanne Willis and Susan Varley
DR XARGLE'S BOOK OF EARTHLETS
by Jeanne Willis and Tony Ross
JAKE
by Deborah King